OLD FAITHFUL

by

The Rev. W. Awdry

with illustrations by
C. Reginald Dalby

GROLIER

Peter Sam and the Refreshment Lady

As Sir Handel was shut up, Peter Sam had to run the line. He was excited, and the Fireman found it hard to get him ready.

"Sober up, can't you!" he growled.

"Anybody would think," said Sir Handel rudely, "that he *wanted* to work."

"All *respectable* engines do," said Skarloey firmly. "I wish I could work myself. Keep calm, Peter Sam, don't get excited, and you'll do very well."

But Peter Sam was in such a state that he couldn't listen.

When his Driver came, Peter Sam ran along to fetch the coaches. "Peep pip pip peep! Come along girls!" he whistled, and although he was so excited, he remembered to be careful. "That's the way, my dears, gently does it."

"What did he say?" asked Jemima who was deaf.

"He said 'Come along, girls,' and he . . . he called us his dears," simpered the other coaches. "Really one does not know *what* to think . . . . . . such a handsome young engine too . . . . *so* nice and well mannered." And they tittered happily together as they followed Peter Sam.

Peter Sam fussed into the station to find Henry already there.

"This won't do, youngster," said Henry. "*I* can't be kept waiting. If you are late tonight, I'll go off and leave your passengers behind."

"Pooh!" said Peter Sam; but secretly he was a little worried.

But he couldn't feel worried for long.

"What fun it all is," he thought as he ran round his train.

He let off steam happily while he waited for the Guard to blow his whistle and wave his green flag.

Peter Sam puffed happily away, singing a little song. "I'm Peter Sam! I'm running this line! I'm Peter Sam! I'm running this line!"

The people waved as he passed the farms and cottages, and he gave a loud whistle at the School. The children all ran to see him puffing by.

Agnes, Ruth, Jemima, Lucy, and Beatrice enjoyed themselves too. "He's cocky . . . . trock trock . . . . but he's nice . . . . trock, trock; he's cocky . . . . trock trock . . . . but he's nice . . . . trock, trock," they sang as they trundled along. They were growing very fond of Peter Sam.

Every afternoon they had to wait an hour at the station by the Lake.

The Driver, Fireman, and the Guard usually bought something from the Refreshment Lady, and went and sat in Beatrice. The Refreshment Lady always came home on this train.

Time passed slowly today for Peter Sam.

At last his Driver and Fireman came. "Peep peeeeeep! Hurry up please!" he whistled to the passengers, and they came strolling back to the station.

Peter Sam was sizzling with impatience. "How awful," he thought, "if we miss Henry's train."

The last passengers arrived. The Guard was ready with his flag and whistle. The Refreshment Lady walked across the platform.

Then it happened! . . .

The Guard says that Peter Sam was too impatient; Peter Sam says he was sure he heard a whistle . . . . Anyway, he started.

"Come quickly, come quickly!" he puffed.

"Stop! . . . Stop! . . . STOP!" wailed the coaches. "You've . . . left . . . her . . . behind . . . ! YOU'VE . . . LEFT . . . HER . . . BEHIND . . . !"

The Guard whistled and waved his red flag. The Driver, looking back, saw the Refreshment Lady shouting and running after the train.

"Bother!" groaned Peter Sam as he stopped. "We'll miss Henry now." The Refreshment Lady climbed into Beatrice, and they started again. "We're sure to be late! We're sure to be late!" panted Peter Sam frantically. His Driver had to keep checking him. "Steady, old boy, steady."

"Peep peep!" Peter Sam whistled at the stations. "Hurry! please hurry!" and they reached the big station just as Henry steamed in.

"Hurrah!" said Peter Sam, "we've caught him after all," and he let off steam with relief. "Whooooosh!"

"Not bad, youngster," said Henry loftily.

The Refreshment Lady shook her fist at Peter Sam. "What do you mean by leaving me behind?" she demanded.

"I'm sorry, Refreshment Lady, but I was worried about our passengers," and he told her what Henry had said.

The Refreshment Lady laughed. "You silly engine!" she said, "Henry wouldn't dare go; he's *got* to wait. It's a *guaranteed connection!*"

"Well!" said Peter Sam, "Well! Where's that Henry?"

But Peter Sam was too late that time, for Henry had chortled away!

Old Faithful

SIR HANDEL stayed shut up for several days. But one market day, Peter Sam could not work; he needed repairs.

Sir Handel was glad to come out. He tried to be kind, but the coaches didn't trust him. They were awkward and rude. He even sang them little songs; but it was no use.

It was most unfortunate, too, that Sir Handel had to check suddenly to avoid running over a sheep.

"He's bumped us!" screamed the coaches. "Let's pay him out!"

The coaches knew that all engines must go carefully at a place near the big station. But they were so cross with Sir Handel that they didn't care what they did. They surged into Sir Handel, making him lurch off the line. Luckily no one was hurt.

Sir Handel limped to the shed. The Thin Controller inspected the damage. "No more work for you today," he said. "Bother those coaches! We must take the village people home, and fetch the tourists, all without an engine."

"What about me, Sir?" said a voice.

"Skarloey!" he exclaimed, "can you do it?"

"I'll try," answered the old engine.

The coaches stood at the platform. Skarloey advanced on them hissing crossly. "I'm ashamed of you," he scolded, "such behaviour; you might have hurt your passengers. On Market Day too!"

"We're sorry, Skarloey, we didn't think; it's that Sir Handel, he's . . ."

"No tales," said Skarloey firmly, "I won't have it, and don't you dare try tricks on me."

"No Skarloey, of course not Skarloey," quavered the coaches meekly.

Skarloey might be old, and have dirty paint, but he was certainly an engine who would stand no nonsense.

His friends crowded round, and the Guard had to "shoo" them away before they could start. Skarloey felt happy; he remembered all the gates and stiles where he had to stop, and whistled to his friends. The sun shone, the rails were dry. "This is lovely," he thought.

But presently they began to climb, and he felt short of steam.

"Bother my tubes!" he panted.

"Take your time, old boy," soothed his Driver.

"I'll manage, I'll manage," he wheezed; and, pausing for "breath" at the stations, he gallantly struggled along.

After a rest at the top station, Skarloey was ready to start.

"It'll be better downhill," he thought.

The coaches ran nicely, but he soon began to feel tired again. His springs were weak, and the rail-joints jarred his wheels.

Then with a crack, a front spring broke, and he stopped.

"I feel all crooked," he complained.

"That's torn it," said his Driver, "we'll need a 'bus now for our passengers."

"No!" pleaded Skarloey, "I'd be ashamed to have a 'bus take my passengers. I'll get home or burst," he promised bravely.

The Thin Controller looked at his watch, and paced the platform. James and his train waited impatiently too.

They heard a hoarse "Peep Peep", then groaning, clanging, and clanking, Skarloey crept into sight. He was tilted to one side, and making fearful noises, but he plodded bravely on.

"I'll *do* it, I'll *do* it," he gasped between the clanks and groans, "I'll . . . I've done it!" and he sighed thankfully as the train stopped where James was waiting.

James said nothing. He waited for his passengers, and then respectfully puffed away.

"You were right, Sir," said Skarloey to the Owner that evening, "old engines can't pull trains like young ones."

The Owner smiled. "They can if they're mended, Old Faithful," he said, "and that's what will happen to you, you deserve it."

"Oh, Sir!" said Skarloey happily.

Sir Handel is longing for Skarloey to come back. He thinks Skarloey is the best engine in the world. He does his fair share of the work now, and the coaches never play tricks on him because he always manages them in "Skarloey's way".

This book club edition published by Grolier 1995

Published by arrangement with Reed Children's Books
First published in Great Britain 1955 as part of *The Railway Series* No. 10
Copyright © William Heinemann Ltd. 1955
This edition copyright © William Heinemann Ltd. 1995